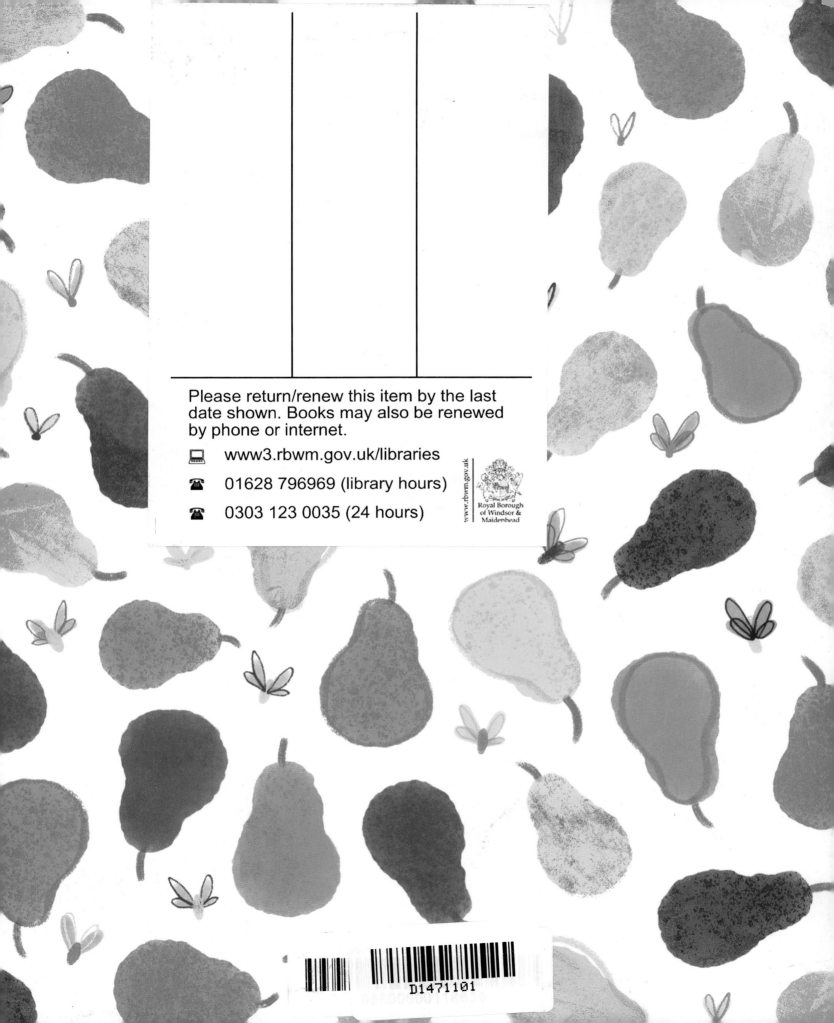

Please return/renew this item by the last date shown. Books may also be renewed by phone or internet.

🖥 www3.rbwm.gov.uk/libraries

☎ 01628 796969 (library hours)

☎ 0303 123 0035 (24 hours)

FAIR SHARES

PIPPA GOODHART

ANNA DOHERTY

First published in the UK in 2019 by Tiny Owl Publishing, London

For teacher resources and more information, visit

www.tinyowl.co.uk

#FairShares

A catalogue record for this book
is available from the British Library.

ISBN 978-1-910328-50-7

Printed in China

FAIR
SHARES

PiPPA GOODHART
ANNA DOHERTY

TiNY OWL

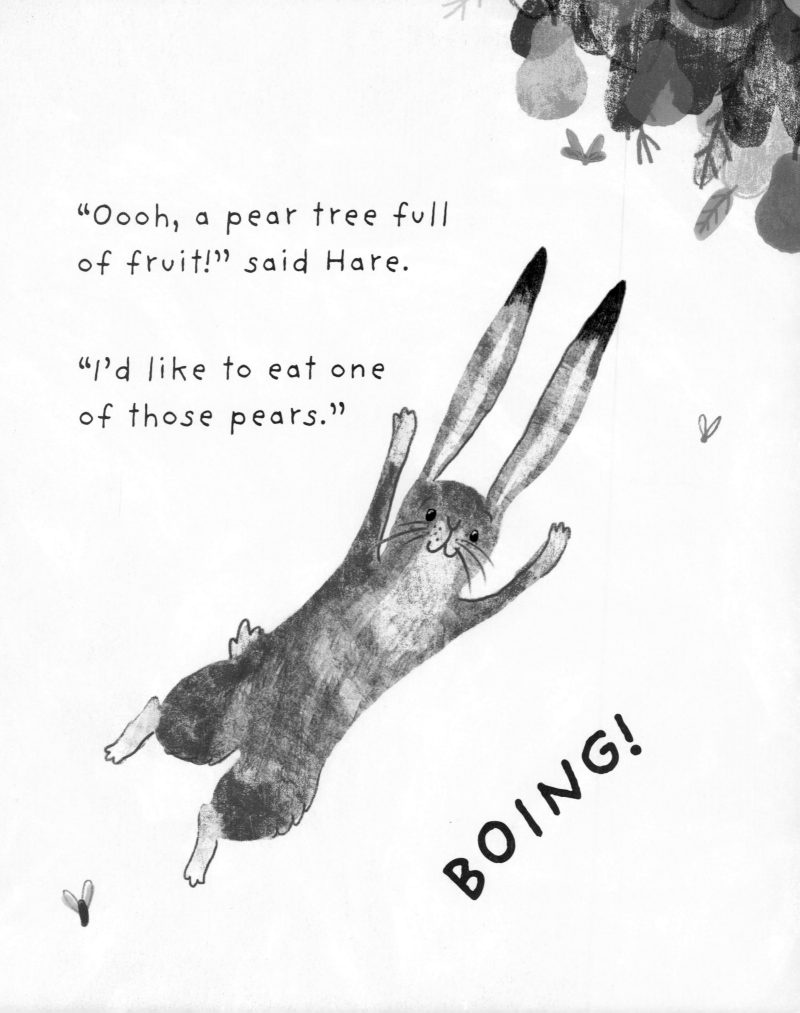

"Oooh, a pear tree full of fruit!" said Hare.

"I'd like to eat one of those pears."

BOING!

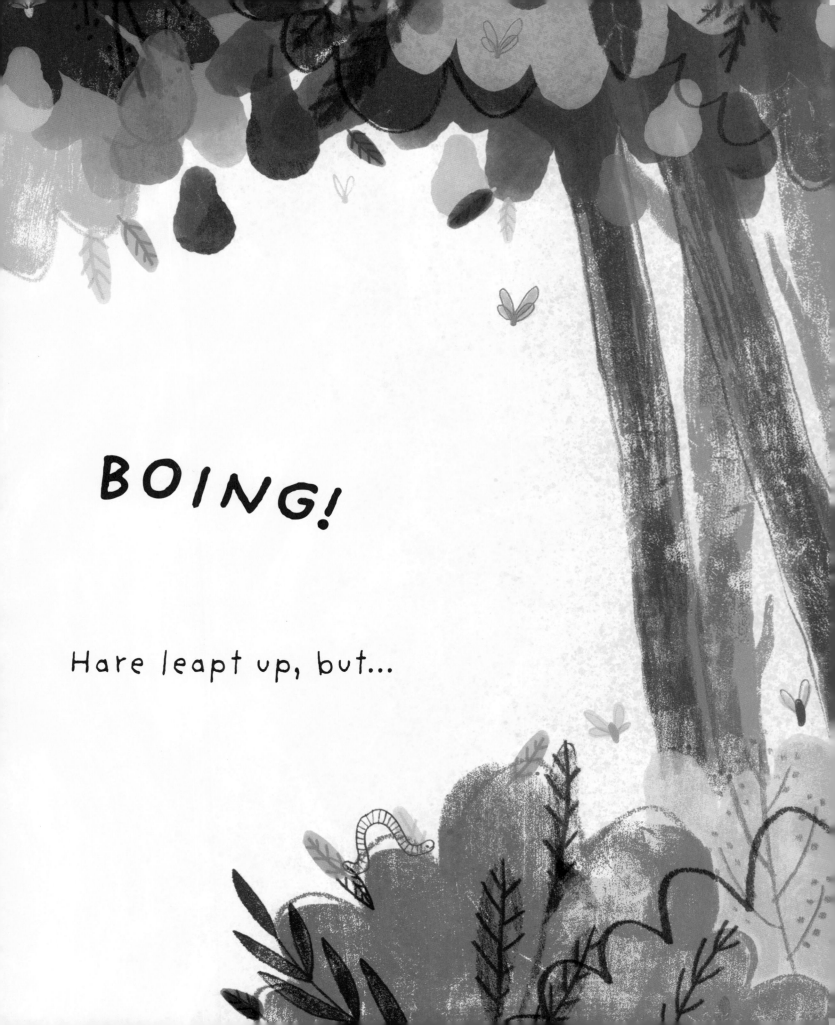

BOING!

Hare leapt up, but...

"Bother!"
said Hare.

"A-ha," said Bear. "I see lots of pears for me! I'll be able to reach them easily."

But actually...

...she couldn't
reach the pears
either.

"Bother,"
said Bear.

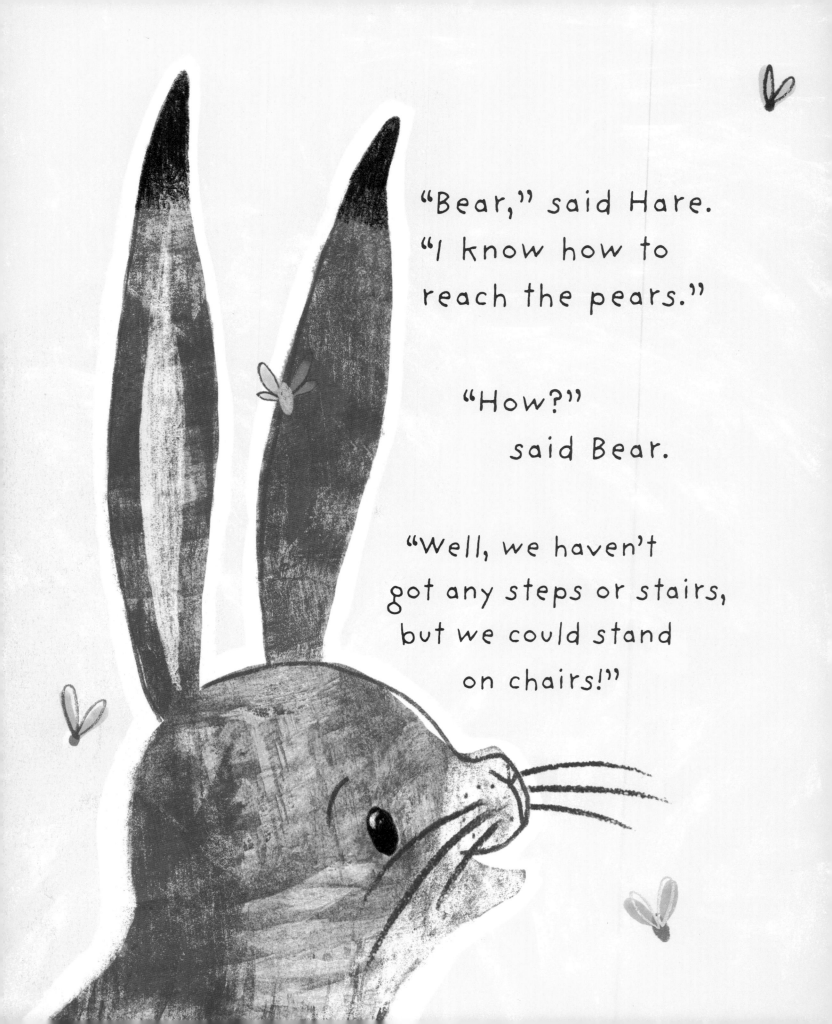

"Bear," said Hare.
"I know how to
reach the pears."

"How?"
said Bear.

"Well, we haven't
got any steps or stairs,
but we could stand
on chairs!"

"Brilliant!"
said Bear.

"I'll share them out," said Hare.
"One chair for me.
One chair for you, Bear.
Another chair for me.
The end!"

"Oi!" said Bear.

"You've got twice as many chairs as I have!" said Bear.

"That's not fair!"

"Oh, sorry," said Hare. "Ok, we can have one chair each, and I'll leave the spare chair over there."

"Yes, that'll be fair,"
said Bear.

"But I **STILL** can't reach a pear!
This doesn't **FEEL** fair at all!" said Hare.

PICK went Bear. **SCRUNCH-MUNCH.**

"Delicious," said Bear.

"Er, excuse me,"
said a tiny voice.

"Who said that?"
said Bear.

"Me,"
said Beetle,
down below.

"I just thought
that you should
know giving
everybody the
same thing isn't
always fair."

"Isn't it?"
said Bear.

"No," said Beetle.
"Let me show you..."

"Hare needs two
chairs to reach
the pears...

...but you, Bear,
only need one."

"That's true!" said Hare. "So it is fair for Bear to have one chair, and for me to have two. Wahoo!"

So everyone was happy, until...

"Uh-oh!"
said Bear.

"This **STILL** isn't fair. You haven't got **ANY** chairs or pears, Beetle. Would you like a pear?"

"No, thank you," said Beetle. "I don't like pears."

"Oh," said Hare. "What do you like to eat, then?"

Meet the creators

Author

Pippa Goodhart

We all get cross when something isn't fair. "That's not fair!" we say. But making things fair isn't always as simple as just giving everybody the same. We are all different, with different likes and needs. I find that interesting and important, so that's why I wrote a story about it.

I really enjoyed working with Pippa's words and characters to bring the story to life with pictures. It was lovely to explore what the characters looked like, what colour they might be and what expressions they had. I mostly work digitally, so I used lots of different Photoshop tools, but I also scanned textures I made with ink and pencil into the computer to make the animals' fur, the plants and the bugs.

Illustrator

Anna Doherty